Those Enormous Elephants

Those Enormous Elephants

Sarah Cussen

Illustrations by Steve Weaver

Pineapple Press, Inc.

Sarasota, Florida

Photo Credits

Cover: ©Kitchner Bain/Dreamstime.com; Page 2: ©Smilingsunray/Dreamstime.com; Page
5: ©Goncaloferreira/Dreamstime.com; Page 8: ©Anke Van Wyk/Dreamstime.com; Page 14:
Bob Suir/Dreamstime.com; Page 16: ©Bananaman/Dreamstime.com; Page 18: © Anke Van
Wyk/Dreamstime.com; Page 20: ©S100apm/Dreamstime.com; Page 22: ©Imagineimages/
Dreamstime.com; Page 24: ©Jens Klingebiel/Dreamstime.com; Page 26: ©Johannes
Gerhardus Swanepoel/Dreamstime.com; Page 28: ©Smelime/Dreamstime.com; Page 30:
©Javier Solsona/Dreamstime.com; Page 32: ©Thor Jorgen Udvang/Dreamstime.com; Page
34: ©Suhendri Ute/Dreamstime.com; Page 36: ©Peter Betts/Dreamstime.com; Page
38: ©Duncan Noakes/Dreamstime.com; Page 40: ©Anke Van Wyk/Dreamstime.com; Page
42: ©Stephane Benito/Dreamstime.com; Page 44: ©Michael Sheehan/Dreamstime.com;
Page 46: ©Nico Smit/Dreamstime.com; Pages 48 and 49: ©Cory Thoman/Dreamstime.
com; Glossary: Antelope ©Galyna Andrushko/Dreamstime.com, Crocodile ©Volgariver/
Dreamstime.com, Rainforest ©Clearviewstock/Dreamstime.com, Savannah ©Ciprian
Salceanu/Dreamstime.com, Snorkel ©Zonefatal/Dreamstime.com, Walrus ©Ralf Kraft/
Dreamstime.com

Inquiries should be addressed to:

Pineapple Press, Inc.
P.O. Box 3889
Sarasota, Florida 34230
www.pineapplepress.com

Library of Congress Cataloging-in-Publication Data
Cussen, Sarah, 1980–
Those enormous elephants / Sarah Cussen.
p. cm.
Includes index.
ISBN 978-1-56164-515-2 (hardcover : alk. paper) -- ISBN 978-1-56164-516-9 (pbk. : alk.
paper)
1. Elephants--Juvenile literature. I. Title.
QL737.P98C87 2012
599.67--dc23
2012014441

First Edition
Hb 10 9 8 7 6 5 4 3 2 1
Pb 10 9 8 7 6 5 4 3 2 1

Printed in China

To My Mom

Contents

Hope the elephant doesn't step on the car!

How big are elephants?

Elephants are big. In fact they are the largest land animals alive on Earth today. You would have to get about ten medium-sized dogs to stand on top of each other just to reach an elephant's shoulder.

Elephants are long as well as tall and grow up to 30 feet in length from trunk to tail—that's about the same as a stretch limo. And one elephant can weigh as much as 75 people.

Where do elephants live?

Elephants live in Africa and Asia. In Africa, elephants live
in many countries south of the giant Sahara Desert. Some

elephants in Africa live on savannahs, which are wide fields of grass with some trees. Other elephants in Africa live in rainforests.

In Asia, elephants live in India, China, Sri Lanka, and other countries nearby. They live in both grasslands—like the savannahs in Africa—and in forests. Some even live in the mountains.

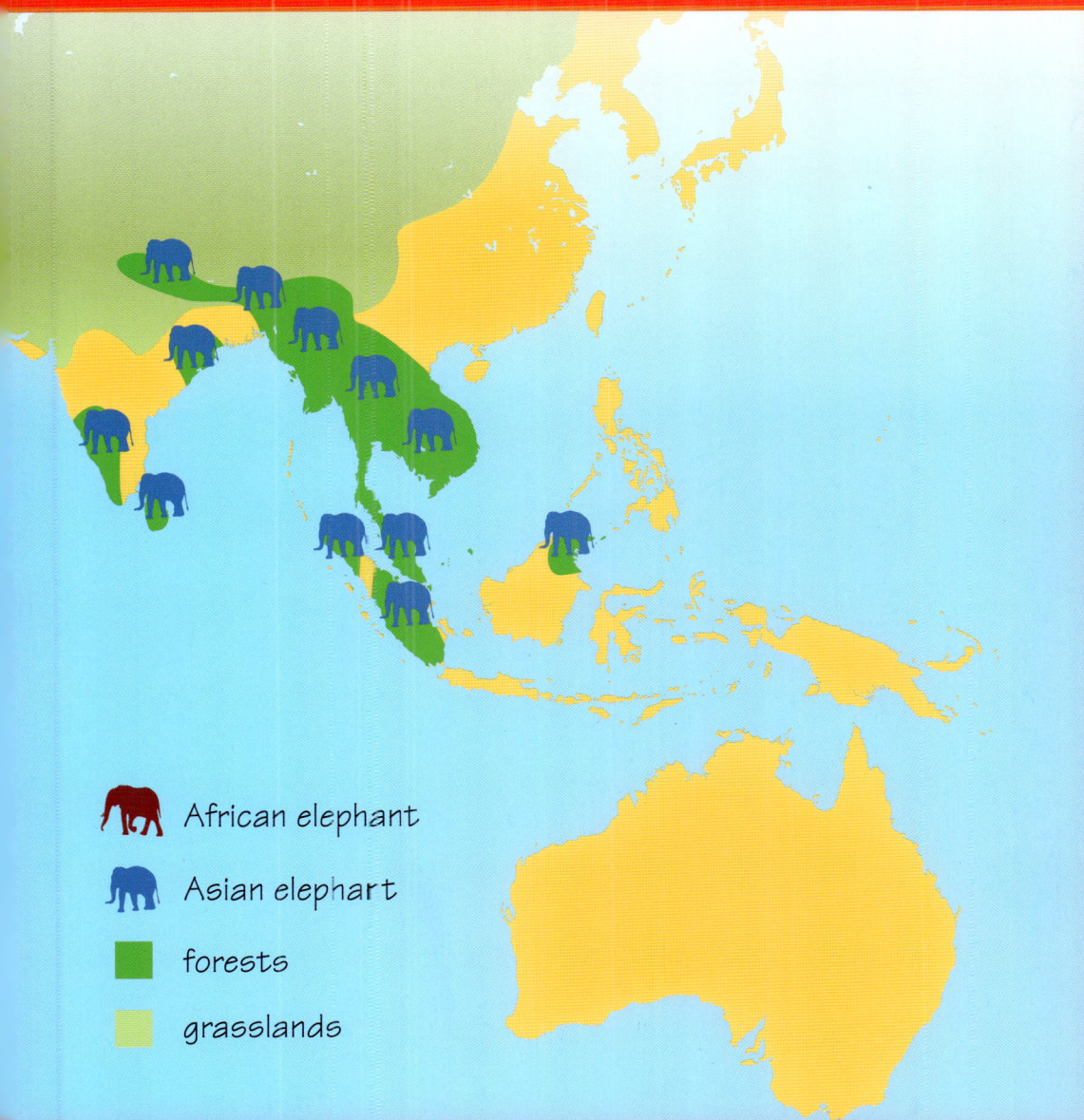

African elephant

Asian elephant

forests

grasslands

African

Asian

Are all elephants the same?

No. There are some differences between elephants living in Africa and elephants living in Asia. African elephants are bigger than Asian elephants. African elephants also have much bigger ears. You can also tell them apart by their tusks. Both male and female African elephants have tusks, but only male Asian elephants do. Also, African elephants are more wrinkly. Asian elephants are more hairy!

There are some differences between African elephants that live on the savannahs and those that live in forests. The forest elephants are smaller with straighter tusks.

If you were a female elephant, wouldn't you be impressed with these tusks?

Why do elephants have tusks?

Not all elephants have tusks. Some Asian elephants don't have tusks. But most elephants do, because they are very useful! Elephant tusks are actually big, strong teeth that grow long. They can use them to fight other elephants or dangerous animals. They can use them to dig for food and water. They can use them to move trees out of their way or to scrape off tree bark to eat.

Tusks are useful, and they also look cool. Male elephants like to impress female elephants with their tusks, to show how strong they are.

If we can protect his tusks, we can protect this elephant.

Why are elephants in danger?

Elephants are in danger because of their tusks. Their tusks are made of ivory, which is just another word for those hard teeth. People kill elephants to get the ivory tusks. Ivory is valuable because it is very strong but can still be easily made into other shapes.

Hunting elephants is not allowed, and many people are working hard to make sure elephants can live in peace.

Can you see any veins in these ears?

Why do elephants have big ears?

Believe it or not, it isn't so they can hear well. Elephants use their ears as air conditioning. The places where they live in Africa and Asia can get very hot. Elephant ears have lots of veins—the tubes that carry blood. You can see them in your own body on top of your hands. When elephants wave their ears, they are actually cooling down all the blood in those veins. The blood then travels all over their huge bodies, and they can stay cool.

An elephant trunk can feel and pick up this tiny seed.

Why do elephants have trunks?

An elephant trunk is amazing. It is like a hand, an arm, a nose, and a drinking straw, all in one. Elephants can use their trunks to feel things and pick them up. They can smell really well, looking for food and for danger. They use their trunks to shake "hands" with their friends and hug their babies. They use them to slurp up water to bring to their mouths or to shower. They even use their trunks to talk to other elephants by making the famous trumpet sound. Or they can wave their trunks in the air to tell other elephants they are angry.

Yum, yum. A twig!

What do elephants eat?

Elephants are vegetarians! They eat grass, fruit, leaves, branches, and twigs. Elephants are so big that they need to eat a lot. It depends on their size, but some elephants can eat up to 700 pounds of food every day. That's about the same weight as 1500 Big Macs. They also drink about 60 gallons of water per day as well. That's a little more than most bathtubs can hold.

Can you hear all three of these elephants purring?

What do elephants and cats have in common?

Elephants and cats both purr. Elephants purr to communicate with other elephants. Just like cats, they purr only when they feel safe. They purr when they are near their elephant friends. If they stop purring, their friends know that there may be danger nearby.

This baby is too busy to look for mice.

Are elephants scared of mice?

No. People think elephants are scared of mice because of cartoons like Dumbo. But elephants are very big and mice are very small. Some people have even done experiments to see if it is true. The elephants ignored the mice. In their homes in Africa and Asia, they probably never see mice.

It's fun to float down the river.

Can elephants swim?

Although elephants are big and heavy, they are very good swimmers. Just like you, elephants can float. Elephants mostly swim with their face above the water and their mouth below it. They then breathe through their trunk, which they use like a snorkel. They use all four of their legs to swim, and you might be surprised how fast they can go. They can also swim long distances without a problem. Some people think they even swam across oceans to get to the places where they live today.

These two males are fighting, probably about a female.

Do elephants have enemies?

Elephants are so big that other animals are afraid of them. The only enemies elephants have are people who hunt them and destroy their homes. Even lions and crocodiles will leave a big elephant alone. But elephants do have to protect their babies. Sometimes elephants are their own enemies when they fight with each other. A male may fight with another male over who gets a female.

If an elephant gets very angry, it will charge. That means it runs very fast right at whatever it doesn't like. Elephants are very big so you should stay out of their way!

The annual elephant roundup in Surin, Thailand, is a big festival honoring elephants.

Can you ride an elephant?

People have been riding on elephants for thousands of years. People have ridden elephants to get from here to there, to move heavy things, and even to fight in war. People still do ride elephants in some countries, and you might see someone ride an elephant in the circus. But don't try it with a wild elephant!

If age brings wisdom, this elephant is very wise.

How old are elephants?

Elephants can be as old as people. In the wild an elephant can live for 50 to 70 years, as long as it is not hunted and doesn't become ill. In the zoo or a circus, an elephant can live up to 80 years.

When elephants get very old, they run out of teeth. Elephants are able to grow up to six or seven new sets of teeth during their lives—just like people lose their baby teeth and grow a new set. Eventually they can't grow any more, and so they stop eating.

This female is guiding her pack down a well-traveled elephant path.

Do elephants have good memories?

There is an old saying that elephants never forget. It is true: elephants have good memories, and female elephants have the best ones. The oldest and wisest female elephants guide their packs for miles towards food or watering holes that they remember from the past. They also remember enemies and friendly faces, so they can let the rest of the pack know if there is danger or if it is safe to eat.

Notice that some of the elephants are wearing "sunscreen."

How tough is elephant skin?

Their skin is very tough. Elephants are also known as "pachyderms," a word that scientists used to call them and that means thick skin. Their skin is an inch thick almost all over their body, except their ears.

Even though elephants look like they are made from old leather suitcases, their skin can be sensitive. They play in mud in order to cover their skin and protect it from the sun, just like you use sunscreen.

This baby comes up to his mother's knees.

How big are baby elephants?

Baby elephants are 3 feet tall when they are born, about the same as a 4-year-old human. But they weigh 250 pounds, about the same as a big football player. They drink their mother's milk, just like baby humans do. But baby elephants drink more than 3 gallons per day. Like people, they are not fully grown until they are 16 to 20 years old.

Baby elephants love to play in the mud.

Do elephants play?

Elephants love to play. In the wild, young elephants play in water holes and spray each other with water and mud. They practice fighting by wrestling with their trunks. And sometimes they even play with other animals, such as antelopes, by pretending to charge at them.

In some countries people and elephants play together. Sometimes they have elephant races, just like we have horse races. And people and elephants even play soccer! There are usually 4 or 5 elephants on each team, and people sit on top of the elephants to steer them.

What do you think these two elephants are saying?

How do elephants communicate?

Elephants "talk" with their trunks and their bodies. Elephants say hello by rubbing shoulders or by shaking trunks, just like you shake hands! An elephant folds its trunk up under its tusks to say it wants to play. It shows it is curious and interested by holding its trunk up in the air. When an elephant gets scared, it will use its trunk to make loud trumpeting noises to warn other animals.

Baby elephants even suck their trunks when they need comfort, just like kids suck their thumbs.

Friends like to hang out together.

Do elephants have friends?

Yes! Just like people, some elephants have lots of friends, and some like to hang out with only a few others. Elephants remember their friends even after spending years away from each other. They also are worried or sad when their family or friends are sick.

Some Elephant Jokes

Fool your friends with these elephant jokes.

Q: How do you stop a charging elephant?
A: Take away its credit cards.

Q: How can you tell an elephant is under your bed?
A: Your nose is squashed against the ceiling.

Q: What time is it when an elephant sits on your fence?
A: Time to build a new fence.

Q: How many elephants will fit into a Mini car?
A: Four: two in the front, two in the back.

Q: How many giraffes will fit into a Mini?
A: None. It's full of elephants.

Q: How can you tell that an elephant has been in your refrigerator?
A: By the footprints in the butter.

Q: How do you know there are two elephants in your refrigerator?
A: You can hear giggling when the light goes out.

Q: What time is it when ten elephants are chasing you?
A: Ten after one.

Q: What weighs 5000 pounds and wears glass slippers?
A: Cinderelephant.

Q: Why do elephants wear pink toenail polish?
A: So they can hide in the strawberry patch.

Q: How can you tell that an elephant is in the bathtub with you?
A: By the smell of peanuts on its breath.

Q: Why did the elephant cross the road?
A: To squash the chicken on the other side.

Q: What is large and gray and goes around and around in circles?
A: An elephant caught in a revolving door.

Q: How do you get down off of an elephant?
A: You don't. You get down off of a goose.

Elephant Puzzle

One day in a country where elephants live, a man wanted to send an elephant to another country across the sea. The man took the elephant down to the port, where there was a ship. The captain of the ship said, "We have to know how much this elephant weighs so I know how much to charge you." But they had scales only big enough to weigh the bags of grain they usually put on the ship. This was a very BIG elephant and would break the scales. An ingenious little brother and sister came along. They overheard the problem. They put their heads together and came up with a good solution. Do you know what it was?

For the solution see page 50.

Solution Part 1: The boy said: "First you put the elephant on the empty ship. It will sink a little bit. Then you mark the waterline on the side of the ship."

Now can you figure it out?

If not, see page 53.

Where to Learn More about Elephants

Good Books to Read

National Geographic Readers: Great Migrations Elephants, Washington, DC, 2010.

Eyewitness: Elephant, DK Children, New York, 2000.

Elephants: A Book for Children, Thames and Hudson, New York, 2008.

The Story of Babar, Random House, New York, 1937.

(Did you read the books about Babar the elephant when you were a little kid? You are never too old for Babar!)

Good Websites to Visit

http://www.defenders.org/elephant/basic-facts
This site has good basic facts about elephants.

http://www.sandiegozoo.org/animalbytes/t-elephant.html
Learn about both African and Asian elephants.

Animals.nationalgeographic.com/animals
Search for elephant and learn about African elephants.

http://www.eleaid.com/
Eleaid is a charity working for the welfare and conservation of Asian elephants.

Glossary

antelope – a horned animal that lives in Africa and Asia

crocodile – a reptile that lives in warm water in tropical areas

ivory – the hard white substance in an elephant tusk

pack – a group of animals

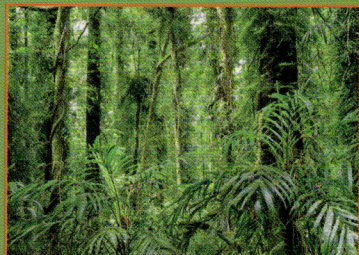

rainforest – a forest in a warm, wet tropical area with tall trees that grow closely together

savannah – wide field of grass with some trees

snorkel – a hard tube through which a swimmer near the surface can breathe

tusk – a tooth that grows very long in some animals, like the elephant and the walrus

vegetarian – an animal that eats only plants, no meat

vein – a tube in an animal's body that carries blood to the heart

Solution Part 2: The little girl said: "Then you take the elephant off the ship and load on bags of grain until the ship sinks to the same waterline."

Now can you figure it out?

If not, see page 55.

About the Author

Sarah Cussen has written, for the Those Amazing Animals series, *Those Peculiar Pelicans, Those Terrific Turtles, Those Beautiful Butterflies, Those Perky Penguins,* and *Those Enormous Elephants.* When she isn't busy learning about penguins, turtles, butterflies, pelicans, and elephants, she works for a charity to build peace in the world. When she goes to Africa and Asia for her work, she likes to see elephants. She currently lives in London, England.

Index

Photographs are indicated by boldface type.

Solution Part 3: The boy and girl said together: "Then you weigh the bags of grain, and that's how much the elephant weighs!"

Here are the other books in this series. Each title in the Those Amazing Animals series, written for children ages 6–9, has 20 questions and answers, 20 photos, and 20 funny illustrations by Steve Weaver. For a complete catalog, visit our website at www.pineapplepress.com.

Those Amazing Alligators by Kathy Feeney. Discover the differences between alligators and crocodiles. Learn what alligators eat, how they communicate, and much more.

Those Beautiful Butterflies by Sarah Cussen. Learn all about butterflies—their behavior, why they look the way they do, how they communicate, and why they love bright flowers.

Those Big Bears by Jan Lee Wicker. Why do bears stand on two legs? How do they use their claws? How many kinds are there? What do they do all winter?

Those Colossal Cats by Marta Magellan. Meet lions, tigers, leopards, and the other big cats. Do they purr? How fast can they run? Which is biggest?

Those Delightful Dolphins by Jan Lee Wicker. Dolphins are delightful in the way they communicate and play with one another and the way they cooperate with humans.

Those Excellent Eagles by Jan Lee Wicker. Learn all about those excellent eagles—what they eat, how fast they fly, why the American bald eagle is our nation's national bird.

Those Funny Flamingos by Jan Lee Wicker. Why are these funny birds pink? Why do they stand on one leg and eat upside down? Where do they live?

Those Lively Lizards by Marta Magellan. Meet lizards that can run on water, some with funny-looking eyes, some that change color, and some that look like little dinosaurs.

Those Magical Manatees by Jan Lee Wicker. Why are they magical? How big are they? What do they eat? Why are they endangered and what can you do to help?

Those Mischievous Monkeys by Bonnie Nickel. Find out where in the world monkeys live, what they eat, and what they do for fun.

Those Outrageous Owls by Laura Wyatt. Learn what owls eat, how they hunt, and why they look the way they do. How do they fly so quietly? Why do horned owls have horns?

Those Peculiar Pelicans by Sarah Cussen. Find out how much food those peculiar pelicans can fit in their beaks, how they stay cool, and whether they really steal fish from fishermen.

Those Perky Penguins by Sarah Cussen. Can penguins fly? Do they get cold? How many kinds are there and where in the world do they live?

Those Terrific Turtles by Sarah Cussen. You'll learn the difference between a turtle and a tortoise, and find out why they have shells. Meet baby turtles and some very, very old ones.

Those Voracious Vultures by Marta Magellan. Learn all about vultures—the gross things they do, what they eat, whether a turkey vulture gobbles, and more.